Annie Matheson

Love's music, and other poems

Annie Matheson

Love's music, and other poems

ISBN/EAN: 9783337874193

Printed in Europe, USA, Canada, Australia, Japan

Cover: Foto ©Andreas Hilbeck / pixelio.de

More available books at **www.hansebooks.com**

LOVE'S MUSIC

AND OTHER POEMS

LOVE'S MUSIC

AND OTHER POEMS

BY

ANNIE MATHESON

AUTHOR OF "THE RELIGION OF HUMANITY,
AND OTHER POEMS"

LONDON

SAMPSON LOW, MARSTON AND COMPANY

LIMITED

St. Dunstan's House

FETTER LANE, FLEET STREET

1894
𝒟.

TO MY PUBLISHERS,

PAST AND PRESENT, AND ESPECIALLY TO

MR. SEPTIMUS RIVINGTON AND MR. STUART REID,

THIS NEW HANDFUL OF LYRICS IS

GRATEFULLY INSCRIBED.

CONTENTS.

CONTENTS.

A CHRISTMAS LYRIC.

STILL, as of old, the wise men scan,

    Before the Epiphany through the night,

The heavenly roof God gave to man :

    O Light, reveal to them Thy light !

Thou, who dost lead their journeying far

    Who learn Thy lore in stars above,

And in our earth, herself a star :

    O Love, reveal to them Thy love !

B

Redeemer of our human lot

For ever since the world began,

To those who serve yet see Thee not,

O God, reveal Thyself in Man!

PASTOR IGNOTUS,

HIS PLEA FOR CREMATION.

" Ashes to Ashes."

" I believe in the resurrection of the body."

WHAT! Do this last disservice ?—God forbid !

Let poison lurk beneath my coffin lid

    To work its direful mischief year by year,

    About the human world I hold so dear,

        And so dishonour me when I am dead ?

Nay! when the Master calls, let cleansing fire

Set free the body of my soul's desire,

　As golden corn uplifts its shining head

　From husk that's slowly burned in earthy bed,

　　Like to the golden grain and yet ùnlike!

I have a kindness for the friend and slave

Which Love, the Master, at my birth-hour gave

　To serve my spirit till the death-hour strike;

　But dearer than the husk the golden spike

　　In full fruition at the last set free.

Then burn my body to the glory of God,

Nor let it moulder under daisied sod

In hid corruption : Love, who gave it me,

Knows well how satisfied my soul will be

   With that of which it is the semblance dim !

Dear dust that canst, as in a prison, hold,

Locked in thy cells minute and million-fold,

   The force electric, moulding brain and limb,

   When Death shall come, as Love has bidden him,

      To call the inmate, and thou'rt vacant left,

It were unkind to thee, poor, faithful clay,

To leave thee to unsightliness a prey,

   A body, of the spiritual body bereft !

No! Fire, the servant, beautiful and deft,

    Shall mingle thee with blossom-breathing

    air.

What! leave thee as a source of pain and fear

To those whose very touch to thee was dear!

    Poor dust, I will not: Love, Who is great and

    fair,

Made thee His temple and for thee will care,

    Great Love, Who seals dead faces with His

    smile!

For, clad in that thou veilest from our birth,

Too human-beautiful for sinful earth,

The body no corruption can defile,

We shall remember thee a little while

With grateful pity, and be glad thou art dead.

Safe in thy walls, we make our heaven or hell,

Betray the Master, Love, or serve Him well,

In years none may revoke when they are fled,

Learn this delightful world, its pain and dread,

And something of its mystic sacrifice.

O Love! O Master! When the pearl of price

Lies at our feet, let no weak devil's device

Make cowards of us, nay, nor selfish swine,

Since Thou hast called us to be sons of Thine,

Immortal, incorruptible, divine!

Let even the body of this mortal life

Be burned for Thy sake, Who its garb hast worn,

That our new body may be bravely born,

Unstained by memories of corruption's strife,

And wrought, O Love, after the fashion of Thine!

THE PROMISE OF SPRING.

O DAY of God, thou bringest back

The singing of the birds,

With music for the hearts that lack,

More musical than words!

Thou meltest now the frozen deep

Where dreaming love lay bound,

Thou wakest life in buds asleep,

And joy in skies that frowned.

Not yet may almond-blossoms dare

A wintry world to bless ;

Still do the trees their beauty wear

Of glorious nakedness :

But clouds are riven with the light

Of old unclouded days,

And Love unfolds to longing sight

His sweet and silent ways.

RONDEAU.

" Lady, I offer nothing—I am yours."
Colombe's Birthday.

WILT thou have words, when silence deep

So sweet a secret still may keep,

And breathe into thy soul from mine

A wordless message so divine

It makes the heart of music leap ?—

Such silence, like celestial sleep,

Hath visions, where, beyond the steep

Dark ways of words, all things are thine:—

Wilt thou have words?

Dost thou then doubt, or fear to reap

The ripened harvest?—Let me sweep

All doubts away : ask thou no sign—

Look in the eyes that now incline

Their silence tow'rd thee! Dost thou weep?

Wilt thou have words?

LOVE'S MUSIC.

(Die Welt ist ein Orchester.)

THE world was called an orchestra : I see

The careworn faces of the men who play

Save when to Love their rapt eyes they uplift,

To thank Him for his strange and heavenly

gift,

And look as though for very joy they pray,

Since, but for Him, the music could not be.

Being Life, He quickens those whose ardour tires,

And, more than all they play, He loves the

players :

Tears veil their eyes when most His glories

shine,

And they who catch His meaning, follow His

sign,

(Their deeds are music, and their lives are

prayers,)

While with His eyes He guides them and inspires.

Then am I sad to know how much is stilled

Before a melody can be divined,

Brave notes that, in their own good time and

place,

May in their turn some other cadence grace;

Mute sacrifice in toiling lives enshrined

That sweetness may in others be fulfilled.

But Love's own heart it is that suffers most,

He feels the pang of every heart that breaks

Amid a dissonance not yet resolved,

And all the tense, wild pain, with joy involved,

When, multitudinous, every note awakes

In diapason, and the heavenly host,

As once of old when love was hid in grief,

Bend down to listen to the choral earth,

And veil their faces at the concord sweet

Where pain and rapture, bliss and anguish,

meet,

Delight and failure, agony and mirth,

And faith diviner for its disbelief.

Love measured once the gulf 'twixt heaven and

hell,

Where clashed confusions of His broken law,

Till unity in sweet diversity thrilled

Order and time and sequence that He willed,

And, through the sacrifice which He foresaw,

The mighty triune chord in music fell.

In music fell ?—In music, deepening, rose.

Through all the unmeasured, boundless universe,

The law of love, in its relentless might

Binding in one remotest depth and height,

Awakened, even in man's most bitter curse,

Blessing and hope and joy's more joyful close.

FAITH IS THE SUBSTANCE OF THINGS HOPED FOR.

A FAITHFUL lover, who has once divined

The very self of her to him most dear,

Much talk of her rejects with all his mind,

Although to others it be proven clear ;

Though good, yet if not like her in his eyes,

He will not hold it true in any wise.

Imperfect type ! who may express the sun ?

Yet broken pebbles may flash back a beam

Of those far heights that never can be won,

Beyond the beauty of a seraph's dream.

Silence is blest, but, while on earth we grope,

Even a symbol may be quick with hope.

Men who about an unseen altar serve

And feel the Real Presence in their lives,

In very worship from tradition swerve

If with their vision of the Truth it strives :

They would be rather trampled and down-trod

Than know their faith a blasphemy to God.

FROM THE GERMAN OF RÜCKERT.

O THOU, my soul, my very heart,

My sweet desire and pain thou art,

Thou, still the world wherein I live,

The heaven that wings to me can give,

The grave wherein I buried deep

My sorrow in eternal sleep!

Thou art my rest, the peace that's given

Straight to my inmost heart from heaven;

Some worth I have, since loved by thee,—

Thy gaze makes fair myself to me.

Uplifted, blessed, in thee I find

My better self, my truer mind!

.

SUNSHINE.

UPON the white and blushing apple blooms

In that old garden where the lovers walk,

And on the cold and silent city tombs,

Afar from talk,

O clean and sweet and healing! On our dust,

On good and evil, just men and unjust,

Divinely common, sent alike for all,

Soft as a blessing, does the sunshine fall.

It kisses little children in the street,

It lights the eyes of lonely men and sad,

It draws new fragrance from the flowers sweet,

It soothes the mad :

Quiet, life-giving, joyous, good,

Warm as the sense of human brotherhood,

To which, since Love's new kingdom first began,

Nothing is alien that is born of man !

AN APRIL SONG.

ROUND the world and through the world,

Under it and over,

Like the light in dewdrops pearled,

Or the scent in clover,

Breathes the sweet and living breath

Of a Love more strong than death.

Grief will come and loss will come,

Saddening many a morrow,

But through all, though often dumb,

    Blessing even sorrow,

Love, that knits the souls of friends,

Makes for all divine amends.

Quench not Love, though pain and wrong

    Smite the dead and living!

Quit ye like true men and strong,

    Vanquish by forgiving,—

Nor in death itself let slip

This life's heavenly fellowship!

A DRAMATIC LYRIC.

Now reigns the joyful May time,

The air is blossom-sweet,

As fragrant as the hay time

When spring and summer meet;

But here in London's very heart, all radiant of

spring,

To a bay as blue as Naples a thought has taken

wing.

I let the Thames go dreaming

Beneath the crowded ships,

Along the Hudson gleaming

My boat her rudder dips,

And under bright, unclouded skies, where all the

world is young,

I meet the faces Memory has often wept and sung.

I clasp the hands I shall not touch

Till deeper seas are past,

I look on eyes that gave me much

When I looked back at last;

And deeper than all reason is the love that under-

stands

And leaves their tangled lot and mine in Love's

unerring hands.

MIDNIGHT AND DAWN.

(MIDNIGHT.)

WATCHMAN, what of the night ?

Wars and rumours of wars !

A moonless dark where the stars

Still keep their rhythmic distance,

With a calm, clear, cold persistence,

Each from the other,

Brother from brother,

Circling for ever, and scarcely breaking

The shadowless night with the light they're

making,

While the naked trees, that are gaunt and

bare,

Image cold Poverty, Want and Care.

Watchman, what of the night?

Hunger and Death and Sin!

Mammon who rides to win,

Steals now, as fiends are able,

His steed from some pious stable,

Vestryman's meeting

His cant completing,

Now with a Puritan rant habitual,

And now as a saint of extremest Ritual;

Cursing the altar, or blessing the cross,

Each heaps to himself his devil's dross.

Watchman, what of the night?

Talk and rumours of talk!

Half maddened efforts to baulk

Satan's play in the city

With a flood of futile pity

That rouses laughter

'Mid roof and rafter,

Where he is daily buying and selling

Beggarly lives in a poisonous dwelling;

Dives rampant and Lazarus stirred

To a newborn hope in his hope deferred.

Watchman, what of the night?

Gossip round chapel and church

Of misery left in the lurch,

Gazed at and made a show of

By busybodies we know of.

Many inherit

The doubtful merit,—

Having made virtuous mild concessions,—

Of the rich young man who had great possessions:

Very near heaven in wish and thought,

They turn in sorrow from Him they sought :

And Love, for He loves them, turns His back

On their pitiful failure and grievous lack

And the shame that His gaze has wrought.

*   *   *   *   *   *

O Love! Avenging Love! Return,

And bid the vast Gehenna burn !

Let death and hell at last be tossed

Deep in the awful lake of fire,—

Beneath despair, beyond desire,—

All sin in flames of love expire,

And not one human soul be lost !

D

(DAWN.)

O CHURCH of God, arise,

And take Thy lamp of love,

The light that never dies

On earth, in heaven above!

With wisdom and with truth

Keep quick and straight the flame,

The light of love and youth,

To save a world of shame.

Burn up the gorgeous lies

That steal the sacred oil,

And bless with glad surprise

The blinded sons of toil.

Rebuke the devil's mart,

The souls in prison release,

Bind up the broken heart,

Give joy and mirth and peace!

Whatever things are fair,

Whatever things are just,

Go, make them free as air

And plenteous as the dust!

In every darkest place

Let radiant warmth be shed

Till in each dreary face

The joy of God is read.

The man whom devils tear

From tombs of darkness take,

And comfort with thy care

The rich, who, moaning, wake.

Tell every man on earth,

The greatest and the least,

Love called him from his birth

To be a king and priest.

Yet keep thy sacred right

   Still at the Master's board,

His table of delight,

   To serve as served thy Lord;

To break the bread He broke,

   (His promise does not fail,)

And fill for guileless folk

   His cup, the Holy Grail.

One day thou shalt be clad,

   Not in a garb outworn

That fools with envy mad

   Devour with eyes of scorn,

But in a vesture white

    As wings of heavenly dove,

All woven of the light

    That is the light of love.

Thy bridegroom tarries long,

    Thy poor are crushed and torn,

Yet, He whose arm is strong

    Will come at early morn.

A TIME-WORN TUNE.

THE breezes sweep like fairy brooms

Over the fire of crocus blooms;

The snowdrops white have left their tombs,

And Spring's a-coming!

Soon will the lilac trees unfold

The hidden blossoms that they hold,

Laburnums shake their clustered gold,

And bees be humming.

O wondrous world, that, year by year,

Grows still more beautiful and dear,

In spite of grief and pain ! how clear

   Thy heavens are laughing !

How sweet the air, how warm the sun,

How bright the brimming rivers run,

Dimpled by fishes one by one

   The sunshine quaffing !

There's many a heart to-day must ache,

Or in the spring-tide glory break,

Though sunbeams all the flowers awake,

   Soft kisses giving :

But light and love may others heal

Until, with slow surprise, they feel

A Master-hand to-day unseal

    The joy of living!

PARTING.

(Written for Music.)

GOD bless you! God be with you still!

God keep you night and day

When you are far away.

My heart your name will ever bless,

My thoughts the thought of you caress,

And for you pray.

Alone I now must climb the hill;

New faces crowd around,

New voices near me sound :

One dearest voice, and one sweet face

That lights for me the darkest place,

    Will not be found.

Yet shall their presence ever fill

    Dull Memory's day and night

    With longing and delight,

Until, beyond this world of pain,

All that is past is ours again,

    And faith is sight.

HUMAN BEAUTY.

"lilied flesh
Beneath her Maker's finger when the fresh
First pulse of life shot brightening the snow."

Sordello.

FAIR shrine and symbol of God's loveliest creature,

As beautiful in faultless form and feature

As some white lily in the sunshine grown,

Or blushing rose whereon the sun is shining,

And over which the dewy winds have flown!

Such curves have silver clouds with rosy lining

Through which the sun, to feathery gold refining,

Gazes in heaven's own light through earth's own

cloud,

So shadowing forth, and through the mist revealing,

The very splendour fogs of earth would shroud.

Sometimes, the source of heavenly light unsealing,

Some tender thought of radiant help or healing

The lovely eyes with wondrous meaning fills,

And all the slender lamp, of God's own making,

With hidden fire of love an instant thrills.

Fair body, of the soul's own joy partaking,

A temple where, at every new awaking,

A Presence burns within the enlightening flame,

That flame of life mysteriously given,

For ever sacred to the Holy Name!

Not sinless, yet, at last, when thou hast striven

To obey the inward light, though tempest-driven,—

Renouncing heaven at the call of Duty,—

In flames, that then leaped higher, shall be riven

The base-born bonds that threaten human dust;

And forth shall flash the strange immortal beauty

Of that Shekinah given to thy trust!

A NEW YEAR'S HYMN.

CONSUMING Fire! Eternal Love!

Who grievest at Thy children's tears,

Yet, seeing further than the years,

A deeper deep, a height above,

A life nor time nor space can move,

Dost light unseen by shadows prove

And with a rainbow veil the sun—

Across the deluge guide the dove!

Soul of our life and of our love,

Thy will be done!

Years come and go and sweep away,

The landmarks that we strove to make :

Through what they leave and what they take,

Build Thou the life that's more than they,

And fill with light of heavenly day

All we have built, now cold and grey

As cobwebs in the darkness spun :

Breathe health into our work we pray :

Beyond the best we dream or say,

Thy will be done!

A NEW YEAR'S HYMN.

We trust not for ourselves alone

But for thy boundless universe !—

Evolve the better from the worse ;

Wake fountains in the flinty stone ;

From fields the cruel scythe has mown

Draw fragrance : when the swallow's flown

And summer's past for every one,

By ripened harvest, slowly grown

From seed that patient hands have sown,

Thy will be done !

Not only through heroic pain

Divinely met and bravely borne,

E

Not only by the crown of thorn,

The loss that touches highest gain,

The fires that vanquish every stain

Till purest loveliness remain ;

Not only by the battles won

Through deadly strife that seemed in vain,—

We pray not only in our pain,

Thy will be done ;

But in the hour of joy supreme,

The gift of powers Thou dost control

When lightnings flash and thunders roll,

The hour diviner than our dream,

That heals our life and makes it whole,

Do Thou Thy will from pole to pole,

O Source of Joy, our Guide and Goal,

 Above the shadow still our Sun !

In many a life's unlettered scroll,

Through bliss of body and of soul,

  Thy will be done !

MARRIAGE HYMN.

ETERNAL Love, for ever near,

Bless Thou our marriage-feast,

And though a human voice we hear,

Be Thou, O Love, the Priest!

Bless Thou the bridegroom and the bride,

That men who see their life

May love the Love in whom abide

This husband and this wife.

Thy love we breathe in every breath ;

From Thee we dare not part :

Oh, triumph over time and death,

And keep us in Thy heart.

At every meal, we pray Thee bless

The bread Thou breakest, Lord,

And fill with wine of happiness

The cup upon the board.

Thou, who fulfillest all our needs,

Around, within, above,

Oh, fill with praise our work, our deeds,

Till life itself be love!

Praise Love, the God of quick and dead,

Praise Love, in Man made known,

Praise Love, the Spirit, dear and dread,

One God, yet not alone!

LE PRINTEMPS VIENT TOUJOURS.

As one who loves may seek to find

Some name by all the rest unfound,

For her who dwells within his mind

    To comfort and to bless,

As though the secret of the sound

    No other might possess;

So we in alien words enwind,

    In foreign phrase caress,

The hope wherein all joys abound.

Is it Winter? Nevertheless

" *Le printemps vient toujours, toujours,*

   Le printemps vient toujours."

If Fortune's wheel, in moving round,

Give us our turn to be abased,

And low we lie, are straitened, bound,

   While storms our treasures rust,

Great Love, Who checks our careless haste,

   May, more than Justice just,

Dull Fortune's eyes, Himself, astound,

   That turn her wheel she must:

We rise above the wintry waste,

With a song that spurns the ground,

" *Le printemps vient toujours, toujours,*

    Le printemps vient toujours."

If some from hope to hope are chased,

Nor covet any worldly wage,

By Duty's sternest mandate placed

    Where selfish hope must die,

Still smiting with a noble rage

    The passions they deny,

With courage and endurance graced

    Though all they longed for fly,

They triumph still from youth to age,

Till Death as Love is faced :

Then, free at last, for joy they sigh,

" *Le printemps vient toujours, toujours,*

Le printemps vient toujours."

BOATING SONG.

DUETT.

Now, thy leisure take !

Sing, comrade, sing !

The day

Has taken wing,

And fled away,

Away !

Mountains clasp the lake

In strong embrace ;

Fair Moon,

Through dim blue space,

Fling, golden, soon,

Thy boon !

Waves in the light awake,

Soft falls the oar,

While, sweet,

Our voices soar,

And mingling meet

And greet !

Glow, Stars in the sky,

Till, deep, the lake

Burn bright,

For your dear sake,

The livelong night,

In light!

Town, where the bridges lie,

With roof and spire,

Bid shine

Each lamp and fire!

One hearth is mine

And *thine!*

THE MAN WHO SAW THE END OF THE JOURNEY.

I HAVE known anguish, loss and disappointment,

Touched the hand of madness, met the hope that

· hoped not,

Yet do I love thee, O world, my mortal

dwelling !

Oh, how I love thee, sweet life that's mixed with

sorrow,

Fain to lose no fraction of thy tempestuous faring !

Still do the milestones spin past ere I can count them :

Soon will the journey with all its strange adventures,

Heaven-sent encounters, sweet coincidences ;

All that makes a poem, vivid, ample, mystic ;

Soon will it be over, and will not be repeated.

Voices, faces, heart-beats, all that makes the drama,

I shall have to leave them : though they are mine

    for ever,

They will be transfigured : I would fain remember

Their poor earthly weakness, dear in imperfection :—

Stay, O Time, thy chariots ; O Memory, seize thy

    tablets !

Friends, who in a cottage have lived and loved

together,

May sigh when they leave it, though bound for a

palace.

Is it warm with memories, quick with life familiar?

Earth, ere I leave thee, parting from my dearest,

Hand in hand a moment, let us gaze and love thee!

*   *   *   *   *

Come, O heavenly Healer, Thou who once hast

dwelt here,

Who didst love those sisters in the home of Lazarus,

And the man who sought Thee, yet who failed Thy

bidding,—

Thou who once didst wrestle in the earthly garden,

Thou hast known our manhood and Thou alone

    canst help us!

Not a radiant angel do we ask, or seraph!

We are not celestial, and we need Thy comfort.

Being God, Thou seest; being Man, thou knowest:

Let us lean a moment, as the son of thunder

Leaned, when death awaited Thee, ere the cross was

    ready.

GRACE BEFORE MEAT.

(Affectionately dedicated to Charles Lamb.)

NOT that the life itself is less than meat,

   Not that we give more thanks for being fed

   Than for the thoughts, the love, of quick and dead,

Or all the gifts of art, do we repeat

The sacred Name of Love before we eat;

   But that the Master taught, in breaking bread

   The grace of common brotherhood is said,

One heart in Love we are, though millions beat;

One body, quickened by one living soul,

    Through every changing age and clime and race,

By death regenerate, while æons roll,

    And light immortal lights the mortal face;

One vital loaf, love leavening the whole,

    If broken, pledged in Love's eternal grace.

MOONLIGHT.

(Written for Music.)

O LOVE, I never more may see

Until the veil shall part

That hides Thee where Thou art,

Come at the cool of eventide

And stand a moment at my side,

My own Sweet Heart!

Come when the red rose, dewy sweet,

Hides in the twilight dim ;

And silver-clear, the rim

Of the new moon gleams on the blue,

Come, tell thy lover sad and true

Thou lovest him !

For earth's glad lovers there may be

The bitter care and fret

Of love imperfect yet :

Our love, my dearest, crowned with pain,

Has passed beyond this vexed refrain,

Nor can forget.

NEAR A LONDON ROOF.

(IN EARLIEST SPRING.)

My bird, still coming, night and morn,

With songs to make me glad,

Unlike the nightingale forlorn,

Your voice is never sad.

No bird of June could sing more sweet

To my delighted ears :

You give me wings for weary feet,

   And smiles to banish tears!

What angel singing in the light

   Where highest joys endure,

Could bless me with more sacred might,

   Or sing a bliss more pure?

What vanished lives have lent you voice,

   And artless heavenly art,

To bid me for their sake rejoice

   And be of braver heart?

Nay, you are just a living spark

Of Love's own joyous fire,

Lit in a world that's often dark,

To kindle souls that tire!

THE SINGLE SNOWDROP.

(JANUARY 20, 1892.)

WELL may we heap the fragrant flowers

Above our Brother's grave to-day !

Death's principalities and powers

Shall never take our faith away ;

Yet may we weep :

With all its care and strife,

A beautiful and wondrous thing is life.

But while the radiant wreaths we heap,

My heart remembers what long since

One told me who had helped to reap

God's field for peasant and for prince,

And felt, amid

The mystery and strife,

How strange the pathos of our human life.

He saw, being to a burial bid,

A pauper burial, sordid, sad,

How some one on the coffin-lid

Had laid one snowdrop, all they had,

God's flower of spring!

With all its care and strife,

A beautiful and wondrous thing is life.

Alike to Commoner and King,

  Come Death and Love ; that snowdrop white,

A poor heart's utmost offering

  To the lone dead, was Love's delight ;

    And Love had kept,

    Amid the toil and strife,

One flower unsullied by the dust of life.

Some loving heart it seems, had wept

  To see Death look so like despair,

Where poverty unhonoured slept :—

God's lovely snowdrop made it fair.

Let a tear fall :

Amid the care and strife,

How beautiful, how wonderful is life !

Long since in Pilate's judgment-hall,

By suffering, Brotherhood was crowned;

Have we no Brothers now in thrall,

Where Love is daily scourged and bound ?

God ! my heart aches :

Amid the sin and strife,

What right have we to all the joys of life ?

And from my inmost soul there breaks

Prayer for our human Brotherhood,

For prince and pauper, whom Love makes,

And Death makes, Brothers. By the rood

Of Mary's Son,

Join hands amid the strife !

O Risen Love, through love uplift our life !

So shall we bless his day that's done,

Our Prince's; and, amid her woes,

The Queen, whose Mother-heart has won

New love 'mid fortune's fiercest blows,

Though hard bestead,

Will feel, amid the strife,

How loss may deepen hope and quicken life.

One race, we share one daily bread,

And if one suffers all must grieve :—

Love is the Home where dwell our dead—

A home no parting can bereave.

Love makes a heaven of many an earthly hell :

By Death, His servant, strong to help and heal,

To prince and pauper He has much to tell,

Which in no other way He might reveal.

Life here is sweet, 'mid care and pain and strife,—

But there, O Love, with love Thou crownest life!

THE SNOW.

WHEN freezing winter smites the whirling globe,

   I softly fall, a veil for bridal maid,

Above the graves, where, like a folded robe

   The worn-out bodies of the sick are laid.

As noiseless as the deepest love I fall,

   As mute and tender and divinely pure;

When sunshine comes, I hide away from all

   In roots that make the coming blossoms sure.

For many a man who must as outcast fare,

Having no roof, and bidden still move on,

I make a bed where he will lose his care

And wake with sweeter words to think upon.

For are not softest snow and fiercest flame

The angels and the ministers of One

Who writes the symbols of His secret Name

In all the universe of star and sun ?

Yet man, who loves, through one heroic deed,

One self-renouncing joy no terrors dim,

More of that Name may in one instant read

Than all the shining worlds can whisper him.

ST. JAMES'S DAY.

IN GRATITUDE TO THE LIVING AND THE DEAD.

OF good physicians an untiring three

Have helped and healed, and, like thee in their

names,

O son of thunder, faithful-hearted James!

Have followed Him who toiled in Galilee,

And served by day and night like John and thee;

The first God took: thoughts that are tears he

claims—

They are such grateful tears that no man blames,—

And two are left, unwearying friends to me.

Thy head, Saint James, was severed by the sword :

It may be harder inch by inch to give,

Through weariness more terrible than pain,

The life of life to the sick, even as our Lord

Of strength and virtue, that the dying might live,

Gave and was weary, again and yet again.

SONG FROM A CHRISTMAS

COMEDIETTA.

HE is a fool who thinks he loves in vain,

Love, lost or won, is still eternal gain.

    Fate cannot sever

Hearts once made one that they should dwell alone:

O soul, what thou hast truly made thine own

    Is thine for ever.

No love is wasted and no light is lost,

Who gives himself, however great the cost,

    Is richer giving;

And those we love are ours, whate'er their lot ;

Those who are dead, and those who love us not

    Among the living.

Lo, loving the unloving here below,

A wider love within our hearts will grow

    For all about us :

Our best beloved are ours for ever, though

Their lives might be as sweet, for aught we know,

    Were they without us.

"THE GREAT WAVE." [1]

BEING a woman, sometimes holy art

 Seems less to me than the sweet poem of life :

 I look at some glad mother, or young wife,

Toiling all day for those who are next her heart,

Or a brave man who in the crowded mart,

 Tempted for those he loves, yet, to the knife,

 Resists the evil in the sordid strife ;

And think how they have chosen the better part :

[1] Painted by H. G. Hine, Vice-President of the Royal Institute of Painters in Water Colours.

But when I gaze on magic wrought like this,

And feel the salt wind of the freshening sea,

And watch the great wave's curling crest rise up

Over the seagulls guided through the abyss ;

I feel how great a thing great art may be,

And how God fills the artist's loving-cup !

THE SATISFIED LOVER.

" Yet, being but a half-truth, therein lieth danger."

OLD ROMANCE.

THE lesser loves that come and go

    And stir the eddies of the stream,

Not love are they, true lovers know,

    But shadows of a lover's dream.

With quivering energy they come,

    With beating heart and restless brain,

Their noisy plea is never dumb

    For passing bliss or transient pain.

But if a deeper love befall,

Enduring love, divinely willed,

Man knows not that he loves at all,

The sum of being is fulfilled.

He thinks he loves not, but his feet

Move lightly tow'rd the goal he sought,

And toil is of a sudden sweet,

And hardship full of tender thought.

The Eternal Love that quickens all,

Our love being kindled by His breath,

Still vibrates through hell's fiery wall,

And at the last will vanquish Death.

And when on earth our souls abide

In Love, the universal Soul,

So deep and silent moves the tide,

We are whole, and know not we are whole.

A SUMMER'S EVENING.

SWEET yearnings unexpressed,

That cannot rest,

Are making music

Full of drowsy pain

And strange delight—

O waken yet again

The dreamy visions bright

That, almost ere I saw them, took their flight.

Joyously sings the thrush ;

Melodies rush

Over my spirit.

Fragrance stealeth up

Into my heart,

From many a snowy cup

Of lilies white, where dart

The mellow sunbeams and fresh breezes start.

Long lines of opal cloud

Rosily crowd

In sunset glory.

Over distant hills

The twilight creeps,

Till a soft quiet fills

The valleys : turmoil sleeps,

And peace divine the dewy landscape steeps !

A NEW YEAR'S SONG.

IF Time were all, each passing year would bring

A deeper shadow underneath his wing

To dark the New Year's vernal blossoming,—

If Time were all!

If Time were all, then, seeing youth depart,

New years would bring new heart-ache to the heart,

And plunge the deeper Death's perennial dart,—

If Time were all!

But Time is but a dream, and Love abides,

Love, the one fact, one truth with many sides,

More loving often when His face He hides

And shadows all.

Great Love is God: through holy bondage, He

Makes all His children beautiful and free

For that new golden year when Love will be

Our joy in all.

"THE RELIGION OF HUMANITY" AND OTHER POEMS,

By ANNIE MATHESON.

Published by Rivington, Percival & Co., King St., Covent Garden.

The Saturday Review, *Nov.* 8, 1890, says :—"This poem has an unimpeded flow, and is obviously inspired by a profound conviction of truth. . . . The poet's gifts are, however, more clearly proclaimed in the briefer poems, in such pretty songs as ' Lucy to Ravenswood,' or the pathetic stanzas ' Memory's Song.' "

The Spectator, *Dec.* 6, 1890, says :—"It is the profession of a noble faith, not by any means what the words are sometimes used to mean, and both language and thought are not unworthy of the theme."

The Athenæum, *Oct.* 25, 1890, says :—"We wish Miss Matheson's book contained more . . . of such simple and touching verse as ' Memory's Song.' "

The Academy, *Dec.* 5, 1891, says :—" The chief poem in this volume is an able vindication of the Christian religion. . . . The sufferings of the poor, the joys of children, the brightness of nature, the pathos of human experience, are echoed or reflected in her verse."

The Speaker, *Dec.* 6, 1890, says :—"Miss Matheson has so succeeded as to deserve our gratitude, and we cordially recommend her little volume to all who know the value and exceeding rarity of true songs of faith and love."

The Guardian, *Feb.* 25, 1891, says :—" The poem is singularly impressive, and invites study. Together with the ' Handful of very simple Lyrics,' by which it is accompanied, it may be cordially recommended to all lovers of thoughtful verse."

The Westminster Review, *Oct.*, 1890, says :—" Some of the love songs, and some of the translations, from Heine and Goethe especially, are worthy of note."

The Scotsman, *July* 7, 1890, says :—" Miss Matheson's work has the distinction of style and workmanship as well as of sincerity of feeling."

The Leeds Mercury, *July* 21, 1890, says :—" Not for some time have we come across a book of poetry of greater promise, or one in which the best kind of culture is more apparent. . . . Lovers of poetry ought not to overlook this volume, for Miss Matheson is not a singer of borrowed notes."

The Melbourne Age, *July* 29, 1893, says :—" Miss Matheson . . . need have no fear when she ventures to take her place beside the humanitarian poets of the age."

www.ingramcontent.com/pod-product-compliance
Lightning Source LLC
Chambersburg PA
CBHW032155010726
47493CB00008BA/2710